# The Moon Followed Me Home

### Written by Shantell Comegys
### Illustrated by Visoeale

Silent Books Publishing
silentbookspublishing.com

Dedicated to my daughter, Dakota, because all stories start with the courage to tell them.

In loving memory of Nicholas, Latisha, and Brian.
Always loved, never forgotten.

Khodi swung back and forth on the swing as her high-top sneakers dangled. Khodi loved to feel the wind between her two luscious thick ponytails and its breeze flowing against the heart and star shapes on her dress.

"Higher! Higher!" a kid on the next swing told his father.

Suddenly, Khodi heard her Mom's voice. "Time to go, Khodi. It's getting late." Khodi jumped off the swing and ran into her Mom's arms.

Khodi took Mom's hand and walked toward the street. As they walked home from the park, Khodi noticed many things that reminded her of her Dad.

Khodi spotted something in the sky. "Look up there!" she shouted. "It's the moon!" Whenever Khodi looked at the moon, she would think of her Dad. They had spent hours together looking at the moon through the telescope.

Mom squeezed Khodi's hand, and
the two kept walking.
"Hello, friend!" a voice called.

Khodi looked up and saw
Ms. Pope leaning out her
kitchen window. A delicious
smell drifted outside.
"I made sugar cookies.
Would you like some?"
Ms. Pope asked.

Khodi jumped up and down and clapped her hands. Her Dad loved cookies. He'd always let her take one cookie from the jar for breakfast—if Mom wasn't looking. It was their little secret.

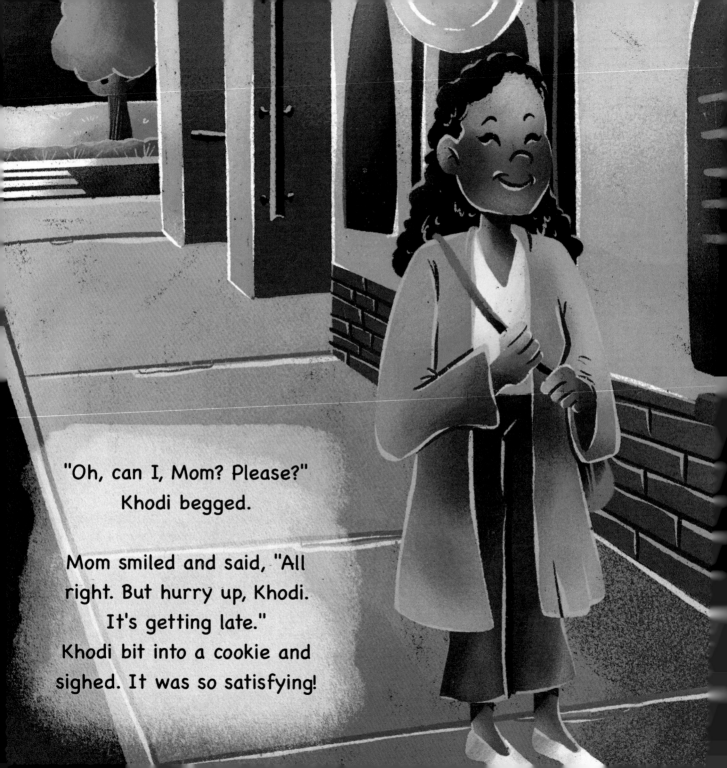

"Oh, can I, Mom? Please?"
Khodi begged.

Mom smiled and said, "All
right. But hurry up, Khodi.
It's getting late."
Khodi bit into a cookie and
sighed. It was so satisfying!

Khodi thanked Ms. Pope, and she and Mom continued walking. Khodi then heard music from Mr. Nicholas's garage.

He was playing his piano. Khodi thought about how much she enjoyed listening to music and dancing around the garage with her Dad. He was a great dancer. She would stand on his feet, and he would spin her around.

"What do you call this song, Mr. Nicholas?" Khodi asked.
"The Man on the Moon," Mr. Nicholas said.
"Wow, neat!" Khodi said, gazing down at her feet. She missed the feel of Dad's feet under hers and how he tapped his foot to the beat. She spun around and patted her feet, mimicking how her Dad would do, and held her arms straight out to her sides as if her Dad was holding them.

"Time to say goodnight, Khodi," Mom said. "It's getting late."

Khodi nodded. "Goodnight, Mr. Nicholas," she yelled as she ran back down the driveway to Mom.

As Khodi and Mom continued home, Khodi skipped to the tune of Mr. Nicholas's piano in her head until she almost tripped over a tiny kitten.

"Catch that kitten!" Khodi's neighbor Brian yelled as he ran out the door. Khodi quickly picked up the brown and white wooly kitten, holding it as though it were one of her baby dolls. "Thanks, Khodi!" Brian said, relieved. "Luna just had kittens. Would you like to see them?"
"Oh, can I please, Mom?" Khodi said.
"Okay, but hurry up. It's getting late," said Mom.

Khodi and Brian ran, jumped, and rolled
around with the kittens as if they
were kittens themselves. All the kitten
kisses made Khodi happy, but they also
made her sad. She remembered going
to the pet store with her Dad to play
with the puppies and kittens.

"Brian! Bath time," Brian's
Mom called.
"I should be leaving, too.
It's getting late," said
Khodi.
Mom waited patiently at the
stairs as she laughed and
talked with Brian's Mom.
"Time to go, Khodi," her
Mom said.
"I know, I know. It's getting
late," Khodi said. She
grabbed Mom's hand and
started down the street.

As they neared their door, Khodi's eyes filled with tears.
"What's the matter, Khodi?" Mom asked.
"I miss Dad," Khodi said. "I miss his hugs and kisses and all the time we spent together. It made me so happy. Ever since he's been gone, I've been so sad."

Mom bent down and looked into Khodi's bright brown eyes. "I miss your dad, too," Mom said as she picked Khodi up and embraced her in her arms. "Your dad loved you very much, and he will always live in our hearts."

Mom pointed at the sky. "Look up there!" "It's the moon!" Khodi said, "It followed me home!"

"In more ways than one," Mom said as she smiled back at Khodi. "I bet you didn't notice those delicious moon-shaped sugar cookies Ms. Pope baked. Or that beautiful song Mr. Nicholas played for you, which happened to be one of your Dad's favorite songs, called 'The Man on the Moon.' And how about Luna's kittens? Did you know that Luna means moon?"

Mom hugged Khodi tight. "Your Dad may not be here anymore, but he is always with you. The moon is your connection to Dad. Whenever you look up at the sky, remember him and know that he is always with you."

Khodi looked into the sky and could feel the love of her Dad. Thanks to the moon, she would never forget it.

Made in United States
North Haven, CT
10 October 2022

25269613R00018